Façade

By Mai Nakawa

Published by Heavenly Fangs Books
charlayne.denney@gmail.com
Friendswood, Tx. 77546

Copyright © 2017 by Haven M. Hawley
Print Edition
eBook ISBN: 978-0-9897685-8-0
Print ISBN: 978-0-9897685-9-7

Heavenly Fangs and the halo/fangs symbol are trademarks of Heavenly Fangs Books
Copyright February 2019: © Haven M. Hawley
Cover Illustration February 2019: © Haven M. Hawley

Layout by BB eBooks

Dedication

I want this story to be for my Grandma and my mother. They both pushed me to continue writing this and listening to me rant and rave when I couldn't figure out what to write. Thank you two!

Acknowledgements

This book has been a long time coming. I've been working on the universe behind this book for years now. Many people throughout these long years have helped me, and to those of you that I fail to mention, I'm truly sorry.

First, I want to extend my thanks to two people that put up with me the most: Cat and my Grandmother Charlayne. I understand I was a very stubborn person to work with, but they helped me so much to grow through this process with both personality wise and my skills as a writer.

Next, I want to thank three amazing teachers that helped me in a multitude of ways. My tenth-grade math teacher that has been a great inspiration to keep going, mainly due to her continue pushing to get this out. My 'creative writing' teacher that helped me learn how to look objectively at my own work and make it better. And my middle school librarian, someone that really helped a lot, and even has a character based on her. All of them helped me in different ways, but all of it really helped me grow.

Lastly, I want to thank some friends. Gracie, someone that helped me so much during the beginning of the book. Felix, for helping me out with writing and talking through my problems with the plot. And Emily, someone that accidentally was Luke. She helped me so much by teaching me how to see through a different point of view. Also helped me with dialogue, my weakest point.

And of course, thank all of you for sticking through to the end of this book. All of you, if you're a fan of my online work or just picking up my writing now, have and will anyway be a great inspiration to me. Thank you for even giving me a slight chance, even if you didn't end up liking the book. I'm glad that I got to try out a dream I've had since I was barely old enough to think. So, as always, with hugs and love, thank you all for reading.

1: We Sit Here

Ryan

I LISTENED TO another fight, another argument, and another crack in our masked face. Something that we've had to wear every day of our lives. I held my brother's hand as we listened to another dumb fight. His hand softly shook as I held him close to my chest. His breathing was ragged. I brushed his tangled black hair as I placed my chin on his head.

He's scared, but I'm not. I can't be scared around him; I'm the strong one. This happened all the time like clockwork. Every time this happened, Father would get violent afterward. I didn't want to start wearing long sleeves again; it was too hot outside for it to look normal. The only reason

Mom stayed with him was that she didn't want to give up that perfect façade.

I hated that people thought that we were perfect; we really weren't. Luckily, Mom and I had an unspoken pact not to notice my brother, so he didn't have to deal with most of the stuff I do. He didn't have to keep a perfect, clean slate. He didn't have to be in anything he hates or do anything he didn't want to. I'm glad that no one noticed my quiet little twin. He didn't need to face the world that I faced.

I always had the spotlight, most people would've loved that, but I hated it because my parents didn't notice him, they didn't feed him or get him clothes. So, I had to sneak food for him, and I gave him the clothes that I outgrew. Father ignored him as if he was just my imaginary friend. Mom focused on everything else instead of taking us away from that man.

I heard a door slam below us; I think Father

was going out to drink again with his 'friends' and his girlfriend. I met her once when Mom was on a trip for her work. I think her name was Rosy. When I met her everything in my soul begged for me to turn tail and run from her. I heard labored footsteps slogging their way toward our room. It seemed to be dragged out as if the person stopped to rest every five steps.

"Ryan? Are you okay son?" She asked, meeting my brown stare. Mom's hair was pulled away from her face, placing a bruise on her tanned check on full display. It was already turning an ugly color.

"Fine Mom," I told her, letting my brother go. I stood proudly in front of her. I wanted to ask her if she was okay, but I already knew the answer. She awkwardly pulled at the long sleeves of her blouse. She took deep breathes as if considering her next options.

"Good, that's good." She pulled a strained smile, "God, I wish that you don't have to listen to that" She whispered under her breath. She looked past me, seeming to find Luke's eyes, but sighs loudly. "It's late; you should get to bed." She seemed to mumble everything she said. She patted my head, brushing my black hair back, detangling it from what it was brushed to for school. She smiled sadly and dragged herself out of the room, closing the door behind her.

I turned to my brother. He was staring at the door as if Mom would have walked in at any second and take us away to somewhere where safe like that's ever going to happen.

She was too scared to speak out to Father.

2: Dazed

Luke

Q UIET WAS A code of life for me. It kept me safe, but it also starved me and hurt my brother, Ryan. He'd always get food and clothes for me when Mother and Father forgot about me, which was all the time. I never did like the label that my parents gave me, that I was imaginary. That my 'perfect' brother was letting his mind wander and created a brother just for him. It seemed if I'm not noticed, I don't get hurt by Dad when he was in his drunken rages. I mean, I wanted to be noticed, but not if I'd get hurt for it or needed to be perfect. So, to protect myself, I hid like a coward. I wanted to have a better life for my twin and me, but with us living in world war three all the time, it was no use.

Most people believed that we were the perfect family; that we were without faults that they wanted to be us! Well, they don't. We had more problems that I could count. I kept telling myself that I lived in the shadows for survival, but that wasn't it. I just didn't want to disappoint anyone. I didn't want to be noticed if all I do is fail. My brother told me that I had to live in the shadows; that way I was safe. But I wanted us both to be safe. Not just one of us. I looked up. I saw my twin watching me, so I walked over, grabbed his hand tightly and smile.

"Ryan? What's wrong?" I asked softly. He shook his head lightly. He places a hand on my check, which was wet from tears I didn't even notice.

"She didn't ask if you're fine or scared." He frowns deeply, gripping my hand a little too tight. I held a smile that didn't reach my eyes and laughed a humorless laugh.

"It's fine. I'm used to it." I told him, pulling him into a hug. "You want to play Settlers of the West?" He nodded as he pulled me to the toy box to get out all the toys we needed.

The bed would have been a better idea, but we needed to calm down.

3: Our Dreams Are Caught

Alice

I WAS A faker, that's all I was and ever will be. I never had a real marriage. Oh, I did love him. I loved him so much that I let everything run past me. We pretended every day that things were fine at home. That Ryan was great, that Luke wasn't there. That everything was okay. No abuse, he worked, I worked, and everything worked.

Yet it never worked. We always fought over the dumbest stuff; maybe it's what we ate for dinner or that it was my fault Arthur didn't turn in something. I wasn't the best either; I tried to drink my way out of everything. I tried to forget that the person that I married and dedicated my life to refused to look at me, except that one time when I got pregnant. My poor boys never should know how much I regretted having them.

My good for nothing 'husband' Arthur left for a drink. It was honestly both frustrating and a wonderful day at the same time. I wanted to leave, I wanted to leave for so long, but I didn't know where to go, whom to turn to. I couldn't risk my boy's lives for myself.

Someone loudly knocked at the door. I rubbed my forehead and stood up to get the door. I opened it up, not bothering to look at the mess that Arthur left. Logan, my dear brother stood there, swinging his car keys in circles. I watched him closely, the light brown hair he inherited from our father accompanied the deep green eyes of our mother. His hair was slicked back and suited him perfectly. He was the static symbol of his company; the CEO of a robotics company that was leading the new wave of electronics. He was only two years older than me, yet much more successful and the apple of my parent's eyes.

"Hey, sister! Is Arthur home? I wanted to go drinking, but I didn't want to go alone again." He asked me. The way that he was swaying spoke the opposite of his statement. He was always quite a drinker, never truly sober. Hell, one time he went to a large company meeting that was broadcasted nationwide with him high off his ass.

I leaned carefully against the wide door frame, thinking and rethinking everything wanted to say to him. "Go away. He's already at the bar. Or with a slut. Whichever" I waved my hand with contempt, still upset with that night's argument.

"You should talk, my dear sister." He responded deadpan, "You only wanted Arthur for child support. I bet you only had children to be noticed as a teen mom." He crossed his arms and smirked knowingly. Yeah, my parents really didn't talk about anything I did. Not until I got pregnant in high school by Arthur while he was in college. It was still the sad fact of my life that I was forced into the role that I was playing for their entertainment.

"I did not" I growled, ready to get this day over with. He shrugged unamused and turned on his heel.

"Don't forget who didn't like birth control."

I slammed the door loudly; the door was used to this abuse. I slid down the door, pressing my forehead into the cool wood that protected me from the summer night heat.

Fights, fights, fights. I fought with everyone about everything to keep what I had and to keep what I thought I had. I wanted to do something. I could do anything. I could easily walk out of the front door! So why didn't I?

Reluctantly, I stood from my place on the floor, dragged my feet slowly to the kitchen, and pulled bottles out of the cabin above the fridge. I sat down on the dirty table that hadn't been cleaned from dinner and opened a large bottle of rum, something that I would move from later in the night. Such was a typical night of fear, hatred, confusion, and drinking. I didn't care if I drank too much. Tomorrow, I would put the cursed mask on, pretending to be the perfect wife and female while pleasing everyone. I didn't care if it killed me; I would let it kill me.

I would rather let it take away the pain of my days than live another one with it.

4: Broken With Pride

Ryan

I PULLED MYSELF down the smilingly empty sidewalk. I pulled gently at my long sleeves with one hand and walked with hands intertwined with my brother. I kept looking down at the ground. I can't bring myself to look at my brother and show him the horrors. I tried my best to cover up the bruises on my check and my busted lip, but I didn't think it worked. I knew Luke flinched at each time he saw me. I knew that he felt so horrible that he couldn't help me and that he had to hide in the closet.

Luke greeted everyone that we passed by while I kept my eyes downcast. He took the lead to help guide us into our classroom. Joyful chatter around the room didn't quit; it just paused for a moment. Some people waved at us while we twisted our way into our friend group. Our friends greeted us all in their different ways.

"Hey, guys!" Hassan, my best friend, joyfully cheered as we walked closer to them. His dark hair was cut short and kept nice always. His dark shirt almost matched his skin though his skin was lighter than his dark brown shirt.

"Wazzup? Why are you wearing long sleeves in such hot weather?" Luke's friend, Felix, asked me. I knew this question was going to be asked, but so soon? Felix's hair flopped in front of one eye. He seemed like the typical bad boy, but he was an honest sweetheart. Freckles stood out against the almost sickly-pale skin.

"I- uh- tripped this morning on my way to school and ran in to grab a new shirt and ended up grabbing a long-sleeved shirt?" My lie was supposed to be a statement, but it ended up sounding like a confused question. I felt Luke tighten his viper-grip on my hand. Our friends flinched when I looked up to lie to them. Beats over silence passed between us, our friends surveying us closely while I prayed to everything holy to let them fall for it.

"That was a horrible lie; you know that?" Allison told me, eying us carefully. She flipped back her dirty blonde hair and reached for me. I flung myself from her reach. I let go of Luke's hand, and my arms automatically pulled themselves closer to my chest to defend myself from some unseen attacker. Luke's face quickly panicked as he reached for me. I wanted to comfort him and tell him that it was okay. That even if the world was against us, we would be together.

Forever.

"What's wrong with you two today?" Hassan eyed us carefully. I slowly moved back closer to the group and pulled myself back into a normal state. Their eyes begged us for information. I bit me already hurt lip, drawing some blood from it.

Luke made his way to my side and whispered into my ear.

"Please don't tell them!" He begged me "It won't help us" His hands were shaking under the glare of our friends. Those were people that were concerned for us. Those were people that I loved, and that loved us. But, I couldn't tell them.

"I—" I couldn't refuse him, not with that face. His eyes. Those damned eyes! They begged for forgiveness for being born! He could set the whole world on fire or cause the end of the world, and those eyes would get *me* to kneel and beg *him* for forgiveness for his wrong doings! How did we have the same face, same fate, the same blood and DNA and yet he used our face to make me throw myself in front of everything that tried to harm him! How was that even possible? Those eyes. That's how.

"What are you two whispering about?" Felix huffed, crossing his arms. I looked at the clock and timed their questions. In five more seconds, they'll beg, ask, and threaten for answers. In ten, they'll give up.

"It doesn't matter. I tripped; that's all." I turned away from Luke and set a dead look. I took my time looking into each of their eyes and showing that my strength would not bow to them. They looked at each other. The bell noise added to the tension in the air around us. These people did care about us. They cared enough to ask why we were hurt.

They cared for certain. They cared so much that I had to let them go.

"Why won't you tell us?" Allison asked, clearly fed up with our shit. I let my finger once again bind with Luke's. We must be strong.

"Because why not?" The teacher clapped loudly behind us, calling for our attention. I turned and let Luke once again lead us away from help and to our seats. I refused to look at the teacher or our 'friends'.

I refused to look at Luke.

5: Stuffed Down Our Throats

Luke

T O SAY THAT day was strange would be an understatement. My brother and I sat at the pristine table during lunchtime. None of our friends sat with us. I expected as much. They shoot us glares from across the lunch room as we ate in silence. Ryan split his sandwich down the middle, peanut butter and jelly fell on the table. I ignored it and used a calm moment to examine the room. Teacher patrolled the room, their backs straight and ready to act at any time. Groups of other kids talked quietly, gossiping to each other about the weirdos that sit by themselves all the time.

My eye gaze over to the other side of the room

to find Mother talking to Ms. Amberley over at the office door, but that didn't matter much in the long run. Ms. Amberley seemed always to know when children were bad or in trouble. She was strange; everyone seemed to love her, with her short brown bob and her plump face with the rosy cheeks.

I poked Ryan and directed his attention to Mother. He frowned. I watched as his brow crinkled, if he kept up like that, he'd have wrinkles by the time we were in high school. High school, such a beautiful thought, a time where we could leave and live on our own. Move to New York City maybe? Live our dreams out to be something more than perfect.

"Why is she here?" My brother hissed. I looked to meet our teacher's eyes. He'd called Child protective services on our parents once, but our Father's brother worked for them and ended up telling them ahead of time, so we'd never get caught and would stay together. I didn't want to go into the adaptive system or go to a family member.

"I don't know. I don't want them to be here." I whispered, blinking my eyes to try to keep tears from falling. I knew he hated it when I cried, so I tried to stay strong. He had this odd thing of wanting to be a hero. I loved Ryan dearly, but I didn't need a hero. He looked to the office then back over to me and smiled sadly. I could feel him examine my face like it was an exam question he didn't know the answer to.

"It can't be good." He seemed to breathe, "I don't think anyone will stop them" Ryan slowly packed up our lunch. We watched as Ms. Amberley walked out and grabbed a mic.

"Will Ryan and Luke Delilah report to the office?" Her voice was amplified by the microphone. Ms. Amberley always seemed like she belonged in a library instead of the office.

Ryan grabbed our stuff, and we stood in unison. He led us to the office, our heads down. Ms. Amberley followed us closely. Before I walked into the door, Ms. Amberley grabbed my shoulder quite tightly for someone who seemed so weak. I looked behind me to find her frowning.

"I'm so sorry about this. Please be careful. Trust the girl, try to lose your family in the city, and don't turn right." She talked so quickly that I didn't even understand enough to form a response before I was pulled away from her. Did she know?

She stood up straight and walked in behind us.

6: Nutrition of a Visual Failure

Ryan

I LED LUKE to the office door. He tugged back once, but I refused to give in. I didn't want to let him run away alone. I knew that he didn't want us to go with Mother, because if she's here, Father is also somewhere. Unless she took it upon herself to take us away from here. No, she would never escape; she didn't want to. Was something holding her back?

Were we holding her back?

"Today, I'm taking you two to the mall to get new clothes." Mother told us, her voice soft and distant. Her eyes were dark and stormy. Something that kills me to see. She didn't look down at us as we walk to the car, a red Ferrari look alike.

We climbed in, throwing our backpacks in the trunk. Mother sat at the driver's spot. She was just taking us to the mall; not to her parents as the T.V shows always says that people do. It's so much harder to escape.

Mother put the car into park. I didn't even realize that we were at the mall so quickly. Her knuckles were white as she turned in her seat.

"Remember, stay close to me, don't bother anyone, and…" Her words tapered off.

"If you see anyone that we know, hide our faces" I finished for her. She pulled a forced smile. It was pained, as everything in our life was. She sat back down, facing the opposite car. I always wondered what went through her head every time we told her things that she didn't want to hear. She looked over and touched a photo that was taped to the dashboard.

Mother was the first one out of the car, then me, then Luke. Everything was always in the same order since we were born. In the hierarchy of our world Father would always be the top beast while Luke and I were so low we weren't even his footstools. As we weaved our way blindly toward the store we always went to buy our clothes; I began to think once more. If my bruises were anything to go by, Father was getting too powerful. Too controlling, too demanding, too much. The leader had to fall. He had to be taught a lesson.

"Luke," I said the moment we entered the dressing room. I could already tell that my brother was looking for possible escape routes and hiding places. When he heard his name, he turned almost on a dime. "We need to do something tonight."

"What?" He asked, his voice soft; he was always so soft on everything. I didn't want ever to see him change.

"We need to run away," I whispered low enough not to alert our Mother. "Don't worry about Mother though! She can escape and meet back up with us!"

"How?" He tilted his head, his hair flopping into his eyes. It was always a complete mess – his dark green eyes sparkled with curiosity. I paused at his question. How would we get away?

"Well…" I quickly made up a plan that sounded believable enough, "We need money, and there's a motel that is on the way to the city." The city. Something was screaming at me that that's where I belonged. That is where we should go. I wondered why.

"Mother keeps money in a jar in the bottom of her wardrobe," Luke said, his head whirling already. "Our school bags should be large enough for stuff."

"We can get food from the party and use that as our food supplies!" The plan was forming slowly in my brain. "And we can go after we do dinner and the normal greeting stuff! At a little more than the halfway mark would do, because people will be leaving, and it would be too dark to notice us!"

"I don't know if it will work" He suddenly seemed hesitant, "But if that's what you want brother. I hope we'll be doing the right thing" He walked to the door and turned the lock to show Mother our outfits for the night.

In the back of my mind, I thought '*me too, brother, me too.*'

7: All We Hear Is Laughter

Luke

MY HEART POUNDED in my ears as I waited for the perfect time to walk outside. I pulled at my long sleeves harder, feeling them rip ever so slightly. I fidgeted all night, unable to sit still for even a second. Not with what was coming up. I was the one that grabbed the money from Mother's rainy-day fund. I wanted to take Father's debit card, but he could probably track the changes made to it. There were only 50 dollars in the fund, but we didn't have enough time to scrounge up any more money. That was the problem with having a perfect time, but not enough time to plan for.

Finally, as the time dragged on to late in the

night, we quickly ran outside. Ryan put a step ladder up and unhooked the lock to open the back. We grabbed our full school bag and carefully walked down the street. If we had run, we would have drawn suspicion, but if we dragged our feet, we would have been questioned as well. So, we simply looked like we were returning or heading toward a friend's house late at night.

We walked far down the street, the hot night air pulling our hair back from our faces. It was closing into summer sooner than we first believed. The next year would be our last year of Elementary, such a grand time. The streetlights illuminated us in a tint of yellow. I pulled on my bag's straps; it was growing heavier by the second. I refused to show that it was dragging me down. Otherwise, Ryan would have offered—well not offered, more of taken—a hand and carried my bag along with his own. We needed to rest. My feet already ached from the ill-fitting shoes that

Mother had forced on my feet.

Ryan led us into the park, probably looking to rest his own feet. The trees around us seemed huge but safe. I wanted to climb them so badly! It always seemed like such a fun thing to do with people you like to have around you. I stopped and stared at the arching oaks that cover the night sky enough to keep the playground from getting too hot in the summer. I grinned knowing that something good had come out of those years of abuse. That moment was the best thing in my life.

"We did it" Ryan spoke sottovoce. It was the same tone we used when swapping secrets in the depth of the night. I looked away from the magnificent sight in front of me and to my brother. Ryan was openly weeping, "We did it"

I didn't say anything as I walked to Ryan. I grabbed his hand and clutched it tightly. I simply pulled him toward a bench. I placed my bag down in front of me and sat on the dark green plastic bench looking out to the playground. Imaginary children played on the swings, kicking their feet trying to fly higher into the air. Crushed flowers pattered around the slides. I just sat there, holding my brother's hand. Nothing needed to be said.

The moment was crushed by a flash of red and the rustle of the tree leaves. Ryan pulled me close to his chest and moved to block me from anything that might have come our way. I watched it with a very limited field of view to find a soft light from behind the trees. I tried to push away from my brother, but he kept a tight grip on me. I pushed harder as two girls walked out from the tree line.

"Who are you?" Ryan screamed at them from across the park. He stood, finally letting me go. I got up, snatching up my bag and putting it on my shoulder, ready to make a break for it. The two girls—both with long white hair that fluttered gently in the light breeze—looked at each other. The older of the two girls lightly hummed as she pulled back her hair.

"You two are Luke and Ryan correct?" The older girl crossed her arms, she pulled back her hair to show off her rose-colored cheeks and pale—almost deathly sick—skin. I felt a shiver run down my spine when my eyes met with the younger of the two girls.

Mirrored eyes. They reflexed my own image back at me; bruised and beaten; even older. I watched Ryan as the girls talked.

"Well, it looks like it." The younger girl whispered, I could barely hear her.

"That's Fantasmic!" The older girl cheered, "I am Angela. This is my younger sister Kimmy. We are your guardian angels!" The girl named Angela acted like she was the best thing in the world. The one named Kimberly looked away from her sister.

"Guardian angels? Yeah right?" Ryan scoffed at them. I watched as he crossed his arms and relaxed slightly. "Angels don't exist. You're just some little girls; why don't you go home to your mommy and daddy?" Ryan looked at me with a false sense of importance. I just rolled my eyes at him and went back to watching the girls. Angela looked offended.

"You little…" Angela screamed; my heart seemed to stop. The air changed from calm and relaxed to charge—as if a storm was about to hit. Ryan stumbled back and hit his knees against the bench. Kimmy quickly grabbed her sister's hand and held it.

"Angela" Her meek voice had a strange strength to it. Angela breathed in and held her breath. The air calmed down, but my nerves weren't going to that quickly. Even Ryan looked a little shaken. Silence passed between us. We didn't want to anger them. Kimmy walked toward us, pulling Angela behind her. "I don't suggest refusing to let us tag along."

"It would be a huge help to bring angels with

us," I told them. They relaxed and smiled. They pulled two necklaces out of pockets I didn't realize they had. Did dresses normally have pockets?

"I'm in charge of Ryan" Angela informed us as she places a dark red pendant on a golden chain around his neck Kimmy walked up to me and placed a light blue pendant on a silver chain around my neck. "And Kimmy is in charge of Luke" Kimmy looked up in my eyes once more, my own dark green looking back at me. I couldn't explain the feeling I got from looking at her. Fear? Hatred?

Doubt?

Ryan grabbed my hand and began to lead us out of the park while informing our angels of our plans.

8: Disgust and Hatred

Ryan

"WHAT IS THIS place?" I asked, grimacing at the door we were supposed to walk through and touch. I didn't trust this nasty place.

"This, my little friend, is a motel," Angela said, doing jazz hands. Tiny golden bracelets clinked together creating a soft bell sound. The pendant on my chest burned at the shake. I felt my heart calm down. I hated wearing this thing. My hand naturally made its way up to my neck, and I gently pulled at it.

"How are we even going to get a room?" I crossed my arms and relaxed my weight onto one leg. My poor feet feel like they were stabbing me. I just wanted to sleep. I could barely keep my eyes open. Angela looked at Kimmy and shrugged.

"Magic," Angela said as if it was the stupidest question in the world.

"No, like, how are we going to convince them that we're old enough to get a room and not have them call the police on us?" I clarified. She cocked her head at me.

"Magic" Angela repeated.

OKAY! These girls were officially crazy! I was done, I was out! Good-bye! I didn't care if I got killed by my father. I was done! I was about to turn around and grab Luke when Angela suddenly was my mother's height. I blinked and looked up at her. Her white hair was tightly coiffed in a beautiful braid with strands of pink, blue, and purple mixed into it. Her jumper was a long black dress that fluttered gently in that night's wind.

Okay, maybe she was an angel. She ruffled my hair and turned toward the door. She swung it open and marched her way to the counter.

"Hello, Miss! How can I help you tonight?" The seemingly middle-aged man asked. He put down the book he was reading and sat up straight in his chair. The room was dark. A poor forgotten plant was in the corner. The middle-aged man had a name tag that read 'Mark.' Mark seemed like one of those aging men that was always at the diner, either for Sunday brunch or Wednesday dinner.

"Two rooms please." Angela stood tall, even though she wasn't any taller than the man while he was sitting, her mere presence seemed to make him look like a dwarf.

"Mh, 'kay," Mark said, wheeling himself over to the wall with hanging keys, "here 'ya go. How long?" He threw the keys at Angela. She caught them, her frown deepened.

"Just one night." Angela daggered in her pocket, most likely for a wallet. I turned to Luke. He seemed interested in the carpet pattern suddenly.

"Luke?" I touched his arm softly. He looked up,

"what's up?"

"I'm just wondering…" Luke paused, I could tell that he was filtering his response to fit one that I would expect, "if Mother misses us yet?" I ruffled his hair and put on the biggest grin I could manage.

"Mother will be okay!" I pat his arm as Angela finished talking to Mark. "It's not even our fault! They made us do this!" Luke didn't seem all on board with that idea but nodded his head anyway.

"Come on!" Angela dragged out each syllable. She grabbed my arm as Kimmy grabbed Luke's. They led us to two rooms on the ground floor and gave us the key. As I turned to unlock the door, I prayed.

I prayed that I wasn't wrong tonight.

9: We Cannot Win

Alice

"YOU USELESS CUM-DUMPSTER!" Arthur screamed as he threw another vase full of beautiful lilies. I ducked, pulling my head down with my hands. The glass shattered above me. I looked up to see his ugly enraged scowl. I choked on a rising sob. I bit my lip and shuttered.

"You're a failure a useless, horrid piece of shit!" he roared as he crossed the room. I tried to escape, but my back hit the wall. Up close, I could see every wrinkle on his face, a face I fell for one blue moon ago. His beautiful hands wrapped around my throat. Suddenly, breathing burned.

I kicked my legs, trying to break his grip. My eyes stung. I gasped for air. I pulled on his hands, begging for him to let me go. My vision became clouded.

I'm sorry, my children. I've truly been a horrible mother. My struggling seemed to be too much energy. He was going to win anyways. He always won. I let my hands fall to my side, and my wildly flying legs calmed down. He threw me to the side with ease. Air filled my lungs. I was barely lucid. My hands were throbbing with a dull pain. I opened my eyes and carefully watched as he walked toward the kitchen.

Slowly, I stood up. My head swirled and the dizziness tried to push me back down. I felt myself rising without any effort as if I was picked up. Gold flashed in front of me. I turned and began walking quickly in the direction of the bedrooms. That's where the gold went. Something in me told me to follow it. The gold disappeared into my room.

I closed and locked the bedroom door. I looked

around to see if there was anything I could block it with. My eyes fell on the dresser. I calmly pushed it in front of the door. I walked to the tall wardrobe, opened it up and looked at the bottom of it. A false floor opened to reveal a pistol, my driver's license, and at least 100 dollars in cash. I grabbed the pistol and weighted it in my hand. I pulled the holster out of the secret department and put the gun in it.

"Oh, my dear Alice." A well-known voice sang from the other side of the door. "Where did you go? Did you follow the white rabbit down the hole?" He was mocking me! He knew that I couldn't stand when people compared me to that book character! But I shouldn't have been surprised. That's who Arthur was, a bully.

I crossed the room and grabbed the phone next to his side of the bed. My fingers flew over large numbered buttons in order a pattern that I've remembered. 555-121-5195.

"Yes?" Jason sounded groggy. I looked down at the clock. It was very late, almost two in the morning. My heart tried to pick up speed at the time, yet it kept being slowed down. Panic—which logically should have set in—had disappeared.

"Jason." One simple name, I haven't talked to my own brother in such a casual way since we were children. "They're gone." I felt my face pull a smile. Why couldn't I feel panic?

"Who's gone?" He asked. I could imagine him leaning back against his pillows, running his hand down his face. I reached up to follow the imaginary version of my brother. I felt my cheeks to find them completely dry.

"My boys. Ryan and Luke. Gone, poof. Without a trace" It didn't even hit me to tell him about Arthur. It didn't really matter if he knew that Arthur was in a complete rage. Or that he had been banging on the door while we were on the phone.

"What!" He screamed over the phone. I could see him jumping up off his bed, pulling his jeans on and running to grab his jacket. "How long? Have you called the police?" Oh right, the police. I should have called them earlier.

"About an hour, maybe two, or three." I looked down at my hands. When did they leave? Could I have left them earlier in the day? Maybe after they changed into their new clothes? When did I last see them? "And no, I haven't called the police."

"You stupid-!" He took a deep, calming, breath. Over the phone I could hear him digging through papers, probably to find his keys. He was never very tidy. "Okay. You get somewhere safe because I know it's not safe at your house" Then why did he never take me in? "And call the police, I'll start looking around for them, maybe call up some of my friends to help. And Alice?"

"Yes?"

"I normally hate you, so don't get hold of the

wrong end of the stick." Click. I pulled the phone away from my ear. The pounding on the door hadn't stopped. I put down the phone and slowly turned. I pulled the sheets from the bed and looked at the window. I pulled at the bottom to open it up. It was nailed shut. I should have figured. The noise from the door stopped. Looking over my shoulder, I placed one hand on the gun. It was still secured.

Carefully, I pushed the dresser out of the way. It scratched the wooden flooring. I frowned at the large white spot in the middle of the dark wood. I shook my head to focus once more. I opened the door slowly and looked first left then right. I stepped out of the shadows and looked around once more. He was gone, vanished into thin air. I reached for my gun again and started to sneak to toward the front door. If I needed my clothes, then I would just bring a cop with me to grab them. I stopped at the top of the stairs and looked at my hand. I pulled my wedding band off my right ring finger. I held it up to let my eye look through it. I shook my head and walked down the stairs, but I didn't put my ring back on.

I looked around the corner once I reached the living room. I took a step out, only to be pulled back. My throat constricted as I felt a scratchy texture burn my neck as it slightly slid against my neck. I reached up and tore at the foreign object; a rope.

"I believe in six different impossibilities before breakfast." A groggy voice whispered in my ear. I struggled to talk, barely getting out something resembling 'you.' "Who am I? I am your *loving* husband" I pulled at the rope. I could feel my fingernails break and my skin tear very slightly. I forgot about pulling on the rope and reached down for the gun. My hand felt guided by an unseen hand.

I clicked the safety off and reached behind me,

a very stupid thing to do, and pulled the trigger. The rope loosened, and I stumbled away from Arthur. I looked back to find him grabbing his arm, the bullet barely grazed him. I stood my ground and looked him dead in the eyes. Arthur was gasping, gripping his arm tightly. My throat tightened around my airway, but I didn't look away. From the corner of my eye a flash of light landed on a set of keys. I slowly started inching my way toward them.

"Kill me; I dare you" He taunted me. His eyes were violent. He had the same eyes as the boys. My poor boys.

"I…" My arm almost dropped. He spoke softly and calmly.

I couldn't back down and ordered myself to get to the keys, get away. GO! Run. Run. Run. Run. Run.

"You'll be the hero" His voice was deep. My legs threatened to give away. I wanted to give up. I wanted to give in to him.

'*Remember Luke and Ryan.*' Something whispered in my ear. A hand twisted around my wrist. '*Steady yourself, breathe Alice.*'

"You love me though; you won't do that to someone you love." His voice didn't tell the fear in his eyes. I finally bumped up onto the table with the keys on it. I let go of the gun with one hand and grabbed the keys. He didn't move. He seemed to look through me.

"No, I wouldn't." I replied, backing toward the door. My eyes on him, I kept my feet moving. I passed the nice white couch. I was so close to the door. I hit a table that had an antique vase on it. The vase fell to the ground and broke water and flowers spread on to the floor. I kept walking toward the door and hit it with my back. Arthur hadn't even stood up yet. I had to turn around to unlock the door.

I quickly swung around and heard Arthur scatter to attack. I knew he was going to. I opened the door and slammed it shut. I holstered the gun and raced for the car. I started the engine and peeled out of the driveway. I didn't even bother to buckle up.

Where could I go? Whom could I go to?

Rosie! She would help! She would call the police and talk for me and she would never abandon or hurt me.

Rosie would always help.

10: So, We Run

Alice

I LET MY forehead hit the wheel once I turned off the car. I arrived safely at Rosie's house. My hair fell around me, messy and slightly bloody from a wound on my head. Clumps of my hair were missing from when Arthur grabbed it. Now with the adrenaline fading, pain shot through my body like acid. My heart thumbed slowly, and my legs were as heavy as lead. My eyes drooped. My own body betrayed me, begging for sleep. Yet, I refused. I wanted to find the children that night.

I downheartedly lifted my head and pulled the keys out of the start. I opened the door and stood on legs that tried to give way to gravity. I slowly made my way up the steps to the front door. The walkway was filled with bright blue lilies.

Rosie had a sister, but back in high school, Rosie and Lilly vanished for three months. Only Rosie returned alone. Her body shook and she refused to speak about what happened. She even refused to talk to me for a long time and bringing up her lost sister was still a sore spot for her family. I watched as my friend spiraled into a depression. She still refused to look in the mirror, it reminded her too much of her sister's pretty baby blue eyes.

I shook my head, bringing myself back to reality. I was about to lose a lot more than a friend if I didn't focus. I trudged up the walk to the door and rang the bell. I listened to the shuffling behind the door. I let my body rest against the cool brick wall next to me. I let my eyes close but opened them back up when the light clicked on.

"Alice?" She asked as she carefully opened the door. I nodded meekly. She laid a careful hand on my shoulder. She didn't ask me anything as she led me into the living room. I never stayed up as late as she did. I noticed the T.V. on, the pause screen of a horror game that she'd played since Lilly disappeared. The word 'paused' blinked and distorted slightly. A small child on the screen stayed still but seemed to blink. I must have really been losing it.

"They're gone" I whimpered as I sat on the couch in front of the T.V. She looked at me for a moment. She held up a finger and walked out of the room. I looked to the side. A small circle of candles was circled up around the frame of Lilly. A funeral never happened, did it? If I didn't find the boys, would I have planned one? Could I even have gone on living after them? What would I had done afterward?

Rosie returned with a first aid kit, a box of tissues, and a glass of water. She set the tissues down next to me and nodded her head to face the opposite way. I turned on the couch, and she sat next to me, carefully taking my head to clean the wounds.

"Rosie, they're gone, everything is gone". I barely was able to hear my own voice. I knew that Rosie wouldn't respond so I kept talking, "Arthur got so mad. We went to check on them after the party. Arthur was honestly angry anyways but seeing them gone threw him into a fit of rage." My friend stopped cleaning and bandaging my face to grab a tissue and wipe away the tears I didn't realize fell.

She reached down to my hand and gripped it gently. "Alice, have you contacted the police?" I shook my head. I forgot all about doing that. She frowned and stood up. "I'll call". I tried to get up and follow her, but she glared at me. So I gave up and looked around.

I closed my eyes as Rosie walked out of the room once again. I leaned back and sighed softly. I needed to relax; if I didn't, I might have gone crazy. I rested my head on the couch and felt sleep sitting in. My body completely relaxed.

I opened my eyes as the phone rang. I hadn't realized Rosie had covered me with a blanked and I pushed it off my chest. It seemed I had fallen asleep. I groggily stood up and looked around. My neck screamed at me when I looked toward the area with the phone. I dragged my feet to the phone and picked it up.

"Hello?" My voice was raw and horse. I barely sounded like myself.

"Rosie? Hey babe." That voice. "I'm coming over; the stupid bitch and leaches gone, hopefully for good, now we can be together." Was it Arthur? I heard footsteps behind me, so I turned around. Rosie looked tired. It was past two in the morning as I later found out. My tired mind didn't take any notice of what Arthur was saying.

"Is it the police?" She asked, reaching for the

phone.

"Come on, baby." Was his voice always this deceitful? "It's me, Arthur. Why are you so far away from the phone?" I bit my bottom lip to keep from responding. He never sounded this way when he talked to me. Was Rosie different?

Who cared?

"Arthur." I mumbled quietly. I could imagine his cold terror, the way he probably held the phone, looking at it, his face confused. I wondered if he looked down at our—his—phonebook thinking, 'Did Alice have a cell phone?' But he wouldn't know. He would never know. He couldn't ever know what was going on.

Rosie looked away, ashamed. She would never put into words what she was feeling. Yet, the way Rosie slumped her shoulders told her story. A mistake, one Rosie hated to have made. Maybe on our wedding night, when Arthur got drunk, and I had to step out to greet people, or say goodbye. I was gone too long, and she was there talking to him to see if he was right for me. She also had too much to drink. She was his last shot to fame, I thought. She was too pretty to pass up.

"I'm going to find my children," I said, turning my back to Rosie and shuffling over to the couch to fall back asleep. I left the phone hanging on the wire. It was too simple; everything was so simple.

I didn't care anymore; that was simple, right?

11: We Cannot Break

Luke

I OPENED MY eyes and noticed the strange room. Afternoon light poured into the dirty window. I sat up and looked around, my back aching from the horrible bed. The room was a mess, and I didn't believe that was our fault. I kicked off the nasty blanket and swung my legs out of bed. I looked around and sighed deeply. The walls were this horrible pale yellow.

I crossed the rough carpet and opened the dark wooden door of the bathroom. The bathroom was a simple toilet, sink and shower combo. The thing that stuck out to me was the nasty, almost yellow tiles that made up the room. I investigated the mirror. My black hair fell around my face. I pulled back my bangs and glanced around the empty room. I needed to cut my hair. I looked out of the bathroom and went to grab my brother's bag, only to find it missing. I glanced up, panic choking me. Most of our money was in there! Where did we lose it? Ryan said he had a map in the bag to where we were going.

I sighed heavily and went back into the bathroom. I couldn't freak out; we still had at least 20 dollars in my bag. Which was nothing? We had all our clothes, at least. Nothing more than that. I took a quick shower. I reeked horribly. I felt like there were ten tons of dirt on me, but there was no shampoo and body soap, so nothing I really could do about it.

I walked out in a new set of clothes and picked my bag off the ground. Maybe the girls had it? If so, that didn't make me trust them any more than I had to. I never should have trusted them at all. They were too suspicious. If they truly were angels, then why didn't they help us more than that?

Panic.

I had to stay calm. There was no reason to freak out, yet. It had only been a day since we've met them. Maybe they would be helpful. I wondered how powerful angels were.

I sighed once again; we weren't going to get anything done if we're not both awake. I gently shook Ryan's arm. He mumbled and opened his eyes. A first, he was confused, but the realization hit him faster than it had hit me. It was strange watching him go from confused to scared to happy back into a neutral state in a matter of a few seconds.

"Mornin'." Ryan stretched and sat up in the nasty bed, "You're up early."

"Not really, it's after noon."

"Oh" He looked around, checking the clock that I saw earlier. "So, it is." He stood up and slowly made his way to the bathroom. I wondered how long it would take him to notice his bag had disappeared.

"Hey, Luke? Can you grab my stuff?" He called from the bathroom. I sat down on the bed silently. "Luke?" He asked again. I looked down to the ground. It was embarrassing. I didn't understand why it was. Maybe it was my fault; I was supposed to be the observant one.

Ryan poked his head out to see if I was still in the room. "Brother?"

"It's not here..." I whispered. He looked confused at first, then angry.

"Where is it?" I could feel the frustration coming from him. I hung my head lower and lower. I didn't want him to be angry at me.

"I don't know." I raised my head to look at him when someone knocked on the door. Ryan sighed loudly and walked over to my bag. He pulled out my favorite tee-shirt and a pair of shorts. Quickly he got dressed and walked to the door.

"Who is it?" Ryan asked, trying to drop his voice. It made him sound like a little kid trying to sound like an adult.

"Angela and Kimmy, dummy." I heard Angela's annoyed and tired voice call through the door. "Let us in before we have to climb through the window." Ryan let out a soft sigh and opened the door. Angela pushed her way into the room, pulling her sister along. Angela plopped down onto Ryan's bed. She crossed her legs and sat with her back straight, while Kimmy slumped over and tightly gripped her skirt.

"Hey, boys! So, what's the plan today?" Angela asked as Ryan pulled out a chair at the table that was near the window. The chair's legs scratched the floor.

"Supplies." Ryan said as he leaned the chair on the back two legs, "Stuff like food, water, my bag…" His voice tapered off. I refused to look at my brother, instead I found interest in the girl across from me. Kimmy noticed that I was staring at her. She blushed and looked down. Angela looked over to her sister, then to me. Angela grinned widely.

"Ah." Angela mumbled quietly. She leaned back on the bed and looked up to the ceiling. "The bag."

"Do you know what happened to it?" Ryan asked, his face lighting up. Angela looked over and seemed to think for a moment. Then shook her head.

"Nope." Ryan huffed and let his chair fall back to the ground as she talked. "How much do you have Luke?"

"He doesn't have a—"

"About 20 dollars" I answered my brother's question. He looked back at me and frowned. I felt bad for hiding it from him, but I had to, right?

"Right." Ryan mumbled as if he had read my

mind. I looked down at my feet. They just barely touched the ground. My neck burned from embarrassment at my twin's gaze. I didn't want to disappoint him, not Ryan, never Ryan.

Leave him.

"Well, that cuts down on what we can buy…" Angela thought out loud.

"We can always steal." Kimmy whispered. I looked up quickly, shock passing through me. I couldn't believe an ANGEL could suggest such a thing!

"Yeah, that's true." Ryan said like he was considering it. My mind raced through many thoughts. Why would we steal? Had he before? Did I steal before? Why were they talking about this? What would we do if we were caught? Could we be going back to our house? That much could get us a cab! A cab, yes! We wouldn't have to steal!

"We can talk about this later." Angela said, jumping from the bed. "The room is about to run out of time." Angela grabbed Kimmy's arm and pulled her to the door. I hurried to grab my bag and followed her swiftly.

"Yeah, sure. Follow them." I heard Ryan mutter behind me. I shot him an apologetic look.

"What are we even going to get?" I asked as Angela led us down the stairs. Angela softly hummed in front of me. I almost put my hand on the railing but pulled it away once I looked at it closely. It was rusted and flimsy. The stairs moaned under us as we walked down. I wished I could grab the railing, but I rather didn't die during this trip.

Kimmy and Angela stopped at the bottom, not even answering my question. Angela snapped her fingers, to which nothing happens. She did it again, and again, and again.

"Damn it, Fallon..." I heard Kimmy whisper. Angela shook her head and focused intensely. Once more she snapped her fingers to look like an adult finally.

"I'll be back!" Angela called as she walked into the office leaving us behind. Kimmy shifted from one foot to another, her back tense.

"What are we going to get?" Ryan asked me. He crossed his arms and radiated annoyance. I felt myself shrink near him. The sun burned my neck, and the suffocating heat nearly killed me. "What are we going to get?" His words were chopped and frustrated. Kimmy looked toward the office. Her hands were shaking. As she was about to run, Angela came bounding out.

"Let's get going!" Angela cheered grabbing her sister once more and headed for the mall area. Ryan begrudgingly followed the girls. I raised a hand to my chest to calm it down. Ryan didn't check to see if I was following. I stood in place, regretting running away, but if I went back, then we would be killed. I didn't have any proof that we would be murdered, but something in my gut told me that Father would be furious.

I forced my legs to walk to the group. They were walking down the main road. A dangerous choice to make, but smart. I didn't know what time it was when we started walking down the deserted road, but I would hazard a guess of about three.

Ryan's back was straight, proud. He was probably thankful for not waking up to Father yelling, or Mother crying, or any number of events that made him panic. When that happened, he usually pulled me closer. Now he didn't have to worry about his pathetic brother. The storefronts around us were busy.

Families and small children ran around, shopping for an unknown reason. A couple walked past us laughing with each other. The female's pregnant belly stuck out, and the man wrapped an arm around her. Kimmy scrunched up close to Angela, whispering about whatever they were talking about. They blended into the crowd. I nervously followed the group.

Together, we weaved in and out of different stores, meeting different people. No one even glanced at us twice. We were just a group of kids going about our own business, and they were going about theirs. I clutched the bag's shoulder straps in my clammy hands, my heart pounded loudly. I thought the people around us could hear it.

Finally, we walked into a gas station, away from people. I followed my brother and Angela into the corner of the store.

"Calm down." Ryan hissed at me. He was obviously disappointed in me; something I never wanted him to be. I wondered what he would say now. "The money, Luke." I nodded and pulled the bag in front of me, slowly opening up the zipper. Ryan watched me impatiently as I pulled out the money, counted it, and then handed it over. He snatched it out of my hand and looked around. I zipped up my bag and put it back on.

"We can't survive off of this." Ryan mumbled to himself. Kimmy and Angela looked at each other then back at me. I shook my head, already knowing what they were thinking.

"Well. Luke, aren't you quiet? That's a great way to steal something," Angela said, her hand reaching for my arm. I backed away, my back hit the freezer door.

"You guys are angels! And you're telling us to steal something? I'm not a thief!" I was offended. Angela puffed out her cheeks. My mind whirled, why would they suggest such a thing? Why were they still harping on it when I already told them I hated thinking about stealing even a single dollar! I looked for Ryan to give me some backup, but he stared at the money.

"We might have to," Ryan said thoughtfully. I stared at him shocked. What is he even thinking?

Ryan looked up at me, deep green eyes burning my pride and will. I wilted under his stare.

"But Brother…" I whimpered under the weight of my own brother's crooked will. He placed a hand on my shoulder, squeezing it tightly.

"I'm sorry, but that might be the only way." Ryan wiped away a tear that was forming and starting to slide down my face. He smiled gently. I forced myself to smile. "Please Luke, think about it at least until we get to the next stop."

"How are we getting there anyway?" Angela asks. Ryan turned his back to me and walked away. I let my head fall, my chin touching my chest. Was I wrong? My brain burned, doubt stabbed my heart, and my stomach churned. He was my brother, my twin; he was Ryan. He was always braver, smarter, stronger, faster, everything I was not. He was perfect. I should trust him!

"We should see if we can get a cab." Kimmy mumbled, but Angela shook her head.

"No, we'll walk." Angela led us out of the store.

"But that'll take a long time." Kimmy looked around worriedly. It would; the next town was about a 20-minute drive. I didn't even want to think about how long it would take to walk there.

"About two hours and thirty-five no thirty-four minutes," Angela said, raising her head slightly to look at the ceiling as she thought about something. My feet ached just thinking about walking for almost three hours! Ryan looked at the girls with a peculiar expression on his face.

"We can't walk that far!" Ryan complained. I nodded my head in agreement. It was outrageous to think anyone could walk that far.

"If you keep complaining, we will have to walk in the dark." Angela pointed out. My brother crossed his arms and looked away. "Look, we're just supposed to support you guys until you get out of the city. Once you're out of range of His worry, we're done with you. So, bite the bullet and start walking." Kimmy grabbed Angela's hand and started to walk out of the door and down the long road that led outside of our small town.

"This is ridiculous." Ryan mumbled under his breath. He dragged his feet as he followed the girls. I looked around and shifted the bag on my back. It felt uncomfortable. I had a few snacks hidden in there. I looked to the side to see candy bars almost shining. My hands grew clammy.

I slowly looked around. No one was watching. My heart pounded in my ears as I reached out. They said we had to steal to live, right? Did we have to? I lightly grabbed a few of the chocolate bars and looked around once more. Quickly, I stuffed them in my bag and walked out the door. I jogged down the sidewalk. Was an alarm going off behind me?

I didn't look back as I caught up with Ryan and the girls.

12: So, We Build

Ryan

MY FEET SCREAMED in pain as I finally gave up. "That's it! I'm done, fed up! We're taking a break!" I called out to the others. Luke stopped and looked at me relieved. I reached out and patted him on the arm. Angela dragged her sister back to us, grumbling about us being slow. We all sat down; half hidden by bushes that grew next to the road. Luke dug through his bag, only to pull out two candy bars.

"How did you get those?" Angela asked.

"I, umm…" He stumbled over his words, he lowered his head, a slight blush coating his cheeks.

"We packed it before we left, didn't we Luke?" I piped up, covering for him. He softly nodded. They shouldn't know it was a lie. But the look that

Angela gave me sent red flags off. My throat tightened up. My heart dug down to my gut.

"Right." Angela looked away from us and checked the road. We fell into a tense silence. I watched as Luke tore open one candy bar and nibbled on it. I followed his movements, but my stomach warned of rejection. Kimmy rubbed Angela's back. The younger white-haired girl looked over at Luke. I wondered what they were thinking. I hoped they didn't judge him. I was curious where he got the candy.

"Anyways, we got to—" A loud siren cut off Angela. "Shit." We all rushed to hide behind the bushes. Luke softly trembled as I pulled him closer to the inside, which allowed me to watch the passing car. A white and blue police cruiser slowed down. It drove at a snail's pace. They pulled over to the side, and two men got out. They left the engine running.

The older man who had climbed out of the driver's seat called "Hello?" His voice was rough and gruff with age. "We heard you kids. Come on out!"

"What do we do?" Angela whispered; her voice full of panic. Kimmy softly pushed us back into the bush area and stood up. "Kimmy, no!" Angela hissed as Kimmy started toward the two men. Kimmy stood straight as she walked up to them with no hesitation. The cops turned their attention to her. Kimmy's steps stuttered for a single beat but continued onwards.

"My stupid sister, people…" Angela muttered under her breath as Kimmy waved at them. They quietly talked to her. Angela bit her lower lip. She clutched her hand tightly into a fist, the fingernails digging into her palm. Fear smothered her features. Slowly, we watched as Kimmy somehow convinced the police to get back into their car. She made her way to us as they drove away toward the next city.

"Nice!" Angela cheered as she pulled Kimmy into a tight hug. Kimmy smiled and giggled.

"No longer a stupid sister, huh?" Kimmy asked. Angela looked away, kicking the dirt embarrassed. Kimmy just patted her sister on the arm and turned to us.

"That was amazing! How did you do it?" Luke asked, tilting his head like a puppy.

My chest burned as Luke looked at them with amazement and respect. Kimmy smiled at Luke but he was looking down like normal. I noticed a small tint of a blush. She shuffled her feet as she reached up to mess with her white hair.

"It was nothing." Kimmy mumbled. Angela looked at her sister; first confused, but then she seemed to realize the truth. She grinned wickedly and met my eyes. A fire burned deep in her. The strange reflective eyes showed my black hair sticking up in all directions and the dark woods behind me. Just barely I could see Luke.

Angela reached out and grabbed my arm and started to pull me down the road. "Come on!" She called out with a sing-song voice, "Time to go." I pulled my arm back as I try to get out of her grip. I looked back to see Kimmy grabbing Luke's arm and them walking side by side. He didn't seem to like it nor did Kimmy. I pulled harder to get Angela to let go, but she just dug her fingers tighter into my wrist.

"Stop struggling." Angela whispered furiously to me. I just pulled my arm in response. I felt her nails break through the skin on my wrist. She wouldn't let go no matter what I did, so finally I gave up and walked next to Angela. Every few steps I would look back at Luke to find him and Kimmy caught up in a normal conversation.

As we walked, my spine straightened. I felt the slight prick of people staring at us. I looked up at the trees, but no one could possibly climb them. Someone would have to float up to the top of the looming trees to watch us. They also would have to be gymnasts to swing between the branches. I shook my head.

It was all in my head.

13: We'll Always Wonder

Alice

MORNING CAME TOO quickly. Well, I it was noon by the time I woke up. I couldn't easily fall asleep after the last night's surprises. Rosie was by my side the moment I sat up from the couch. She handed me a plate full of cold waffles with strawberries placed randomly around the plate. Together, we ate in complete silence. I couldn't force myself to talk to her.

Once I finished my food, Rosie took the empty plate from my hands and went to the kitchen. I stood up and walked to the window. Did the boys head home? Had there been any progress in the investigation? Horrors of what would happen if they went home without me there. Rosie tapped my shoulder lightly, shaking me out of thoughts.

"Alice, I just want to say…" Her voice was soft and full of regret.

"What?" Ouch, that came out too harsh. I watched as Rosie slightly recoiled but she still sat down next to me. For a few moments, the tension only grew. I shouldn't have snapped at her.

"I'm so sorry." She mumbled, "I know, it's way too late to say I'm sorry. But, please Alice. I promise. It only happened once." She pulled and twisted her shirt. Pale skin was shown under the now wrinkled shirt. My mind was tired, what should I have said? The silence only grew as I didn't answer, and she didn't add anything else. Suddenly, the phone cut through our uncomfortable silence. As we both jumped up, I pushed past Rosie to grab the phone. She watched me with pitying eyes as I yanked the phone from the wall and held it tightly to my ear.

"Hello?" I asked, hope tightened my chest and I

barely recognized my high pitched voice. Rosie placed a hand on my shoulder and leaned in to listen to what was said.

"Hello? This is Detective Vondila Perdita from the New York State Police Department." The female voice on the other end of the line was sweet, "We are looking for Mrs. Alice Delilah."

"Yes! I'm Alice! Have you found my boys?" I frantically asked. I wanted to push past all the expected stuff and all the formalities. I just wanted my boys back.

"I'm sorry to say that we have yet to locate your children, Mrs. Delilah. There has been progress with the investigation, however. All units in the surrounding area are on High Alert and an AMBER ALERT has been issued statewide." My heart nearly exploded as I listened closely to the other side of the line, "Given the length of time that they have been missing, we suspect that they may not be in town, but in a surrounding city.

They may have slipped past us."

"What do we do now?" I asked. A tear ran down my check. My head pounded. Everything in me screamed to just go back to bed. Don't wake up. Don't move.

"Ma'am, please bear in mind this just a possibility. This department along with others in the county treats cases with missing children with the highest priority." Detective Perdita spoke with the soft voice that a mother would use with a young child.

"Okay…" Where will we look? New York City? Maybe they went there? Ryan always liked the bright lights and the tall buildings. Luke liked the parks, but he hated how many people were there. Should I go look there?

Yes, There. They're there.

"Ma'am, I will personally reassure you that we will try everything to find your children. Please stay close to the phone." I nodded, even though she wouldn't be able to see me.

"Okay," I mumbled, "Thank you." I hung up the phone. I slowly put it back on the wall and hugged my arms closely around myself. Rosie tried to hug me, but I shrugged her off. I couldn't just stay there feeling sorry for myself. I needed to find my kids! Slowly, I breathed in and out. I straightened out my back and lifted my head up to face Rosie.

"I'm going out to find them," I told her, my tone leaving no room for arguments. My friend opened her mouth to protest but closed it again. She barely nodded. I turned and walked to the end table. The candles and the picture of Lilly from the previous night were gone. I snatched my keys off the top and marched out of the door.

As I sat in my driver's seat, doubt ran through me. I turned the key to start the engine and held my head higher than before. No, I couldn't let anything stop me right now. I knew where I had to go.

It was just a matter of timing and fate.

14: If We'll Survive

Ryan

"LUKE ARE YOU all right?" I slowed down to get next to Luke, pushing Kimmy out of the way. My arm was still marked by Angela's nails. It's been two hours and it almost seemed like we weren't any closer to the city. We already ate all our food. My feet burned, and my legs felt like lead every time we paused for even a short time. My jeans were stained with dirt with as often as we had to dodge the cars that we either zooming past or slowed down to check if their eyes had really seen a group of kids walking down the lonely road.

"Ryan, I'm scared." He spoke softly. The silence was like a glass too precious to break. I looked away from Luke to the two girls in front of us as I thought of something to say. The girls kept a solid grip on their long hair. Kimmy pressed one hand on her skirt to keep it down, while Angela dug around in her pocket for rubber bands. I only looked back to Luke when I felt his hand slip into my own.

"Of what?" I asked, tightening my grip on his hand. He stayed quiet, so I did too.

"Of everything I guess," Luke mumbled under his breath.

"I'm here!" I told him. "So, don't worry!"

"What about Mother?" He asked loudly, and my automatic reaction was to squeeze his hand. Fear closed my throat. He looked at me with pitiful eyes. Those damned eyes!

"She's an adult. She'll be fine" I muttered, annoyed that we were even talking about her. I nearly prayed: *"Just make him stop looking at me. Stop it. Stop it."*

"What if she isn't though, what happens then? What if we end up going back to find her dead?

What if?" He wailed, drawing the attention of the girls. Why did he even think about her?

"Luke" My voice warned him to quiet down, "She'll be fine. If not, we have each other." Luke looked down. I sighed heavily and let go of his hand to wrap my arm around him. "Just forget about her for now." He looked away finally. I didn't have to feel his gaze.

"Okay, Ryan." He said, looking at the stars.

"Luke." I rubbed his arm. Luke just kept walking, watching the stars and the treetops. I once again sighed and let my arm fall to my side. I messed up, I guessed. He was mad at me now. Great.

I watched his face for any twinge of anything else besides regret. Luke just didn't see it my way. The girls kept walking, if not a bit faster. They probably thought I was right, didn't they? They believed me.

Luke just needed time to think that through to realize that I was right.

15: Probably Not

Luke

THE LIGHTS OF the city were always grand. The night was illumined from high above, casting golden lights down upon us. The streets were filled with adults heading to places. Men were talking in the corner. They were all quiet, but the untimed shuffling of their feet caused a noise that I had never liked. I looked around; the buildings loomed above us.

"Hey, guys," Angela called. I turned around to see Angela looking around frantically. "So, um. We forgot something." I looked at her confused. What was going on?

"We have to leave for a while." Kimmy walked over to her sister. Things clicked slowly. They completed what they needed to. They didn't have to stay any longer. I clenched my fists tightly. I couldn't believe what I heard.

"Why?" I asked them. Wait, why did I care? "Ryan! Tell them to stay!" I looked over to my brother to only find him smiling. Smiling, for God's sake! I felt anger nearly breaking my bones, releasing hot lava in me.

"Sorry, Luke. They have to." Ryan's smile fell, and he frowned at me. He was lying to me in my face! I couldn't believe any of this! They couldn't leave! Ryan couldn't lie to me.

"It's not our choice," Angela said frowning. Lies. Unfair. They couldn't do this to me.

"You can't leave us; that's not fair!" I desperately screamed, pulling the attention of another passer-by. Ryan grabbed my arm trying to quiet me down, but I pushed him off. "What's next? You're going to leave me too?" I pushed Ryan farther away from me.

Run

"Hey! It's not my fault!" He snapped at me. He took a step toward me, but I stood my ground. I couldn't do this! I was scared! I couldn't do this!

"Yes, it is!" I cried out. What was I doing? What was I saying? This wasn't me. I had to say I was sorry. It was Ryan; he just wanted the best for me. "Who thought of this insane plan? You! You're always dragging me to do stuff I don't want to!" I shouted at my brother.

"What are you talking about, Luke?" Ryan asked, really confused. I felt tears burning my eyes. My skin boiled, and my heart pounded louder and louder in my ears.

"I'm talking about literally our entire lives you've been making me do the things you want to! I want a blue shirt, and you choose the black one! I want to play Aliens, and you make me play Settlers of the West! I can't stand you, Ryan!" I felt the lie burn my tongue and scratch my throat.

"If you hate me so much then leave!" Ryan screamed back. My throat tightened up.

Every part of my body was shaking hard. I could barely see through my tears. I hung my head; I was supposed to leave. I was nothing. "Luke, wait I didn't—" I took off the alley that was next to us. I pushed past the men. I ran as hard as I could. The alley was straight away, but finally, I had to stop. I looked left and right. Where was I supposed to go? Left, or right?

I took off the right way.

My feet finally betrayed me in the middle of a small park. I collapsed to the ground, panting and begging for a re-do. I shouldn't have said any of that! What was I thinking? God, what was Ryan saying?

I looked up to find the swing set swaying in the soft wind. The slides were barren. Everything was just downright creepy. Why was there a park near alleyways? I felt my eyelids droop. My feet ached in a way that made me think I could never run again.

I made my way to a bench overlooking the park. I took off my backpack and set it next to me. I slowly undid the laces of my sneakers. Relief flooded through me as I took off my shoes and rubbed the bottom of my feet.

I smiled softly and relaxed into the surprisingly comfortable wooden bench. I closed my eyes for a second only to feel dread filling my stomach. Quickly I opened my eyes and looked around wildly.

"Hello, young man. Are you lost?"

16: We Will Fail

Alice

T HE ROAD WAS too long, the speed limit too slow, the trees too big. I wished that I could shrink everything down to a smaller scale. That would have made everything so much easier. I had been able to find Luke and Ryan without any problems. I could have picked them out of the millions of small people running around. I could have held them in my pocket and loved them. I could have placed them in a safe cage with everything they ever needed or wanted.

I gripped the wheel of the car tighter. My knuckles turned white and the leather crinkled underneath my grip. Everything would have been so much easier if the world had been in my pocket and I didn't have to worry about others. I wondered where they went. I didn't even know where I was heading. To the city, I believed; New York City with its lights, the sounds, the people. Everything there was wonderfully boring.

I let my gut drive as my mind wandered into territory that I didn't enter since childhood. I imagined a life full of happiness and joy. I would have married my high school sweetheart, and he would have loved me. I would have had two beautiful children that would have had the world handed to them on a silver platter. They would have laughed, and cried, and said 'I love you, Mommy!' every day. I would have been happy. My husband would have treated me to flowers and candy. I would have baked cakes and pies and cooked dinner. And after we had gotten home from work and ate as a family and the children went to bed, then we would have made love.

That life would have been so sweet. I would

have loved it; one son and one daughter. Yet, instead, I got this. I got a high school sweetheart that failed out of college. I had children when I just turned nineteen. Twin boys, both of whom I love deeply. I begged for my sweetheart to live with me or at least pay child support. Then the wrath he brought upon my life. The fear and hiding. The nights alone in tears, clutching my children to my chest.

Yet I stayed in the lies! I made my bed in a monster's nest. I brought children into a world that hates and burns and rapes happiness and joy and everything in between. I stayed with him as he beat me black and blue as he ravaged my mind and made me question everything that made me a human.

I never told anyone. My brother and Rosie found out by themselves. But no one was told. I was just clumsy. I had kids. I would 'trip' over their toys.

For days, months, years even. To everyone around him, he was the sweetest man, loving husband, fantastic father, but I knew better. I never stood up to him. I never left, never told the kids where to go. I just stared and watched as my life decayed and the masquerade grew larger every day.

The kids found the courage that had been beaten out of me. They took the bad with the worse and decided to take themselves out of a horrible place. So, they ran away, and yet I was going to drag them back. No, I was going to take them away from that man. I planned to find a new place, it may have been smaller, but it was going to work. Maybe we could move back to my hometown. I wouldn't let that man touch my children again.

I wouldn't let that man hurt anyone anymore.

17: But Once I Leave

Ryan

I STOOD THERE forever. I was trying to process what just happened. The girls were stunned, disbelief covered their faces. I finally cried out his name and followed him, the girls racing after me.

I saw his black hair go in and out of view. I strained my voice, calling after him. I was in tears as we ran. The rain pelted us like the stabs of guilt that ran through my heart. What was I thinking? I was not supposed to hurt him in any way.

My chest began to burn, and it felt like someone just sat down on top of me. Jesus, that again? Why did that always happen? I gasped for air and begged my legs to keep running. I needed to catch my brother. I silently let out a prayer as my legs seemed to slow down. Please, I needed to run faster!

I finally stopped at a crossroad. I lost him. I looked left and right, where was I to go? I doubled over and tried to breathe deeply. Sweat dripped down into my eyes causing me to reach up and rub at them. My mind was muddled with exhaustion at that point. My legs weighted me down like the ground was suddenly made of water, and I was going to drown. Angela and Kimmy caught up with me and began looking side to side.

"Where did he go?" Angela asked, grabbing my shoulders and shaking me harshly. I opened my mouth to respond, but my throat closed. "Ugh, never mind!" She pushed me away, my back hit the brick wall, and I slid down. She clasped her hands together and mumbled soft prayers as I did as I was running. I watched her slowly look up to the sky, her eyes fluttering open to reveal silver that shimmered similar to the metal. She suddenly dropped her hands and looked back at me; her eyes normal. Something was off though. They didn't reflect me back, only my surroundings.

"Let's go" She ran toward the left path, but something in me screamed to run to the right. I got up, my head spinning. Fatigue was momentarily forgotten as I took down the right path. The only sound I could hear was the pounding of my feet. Doubt plagued my mind as I kept running and didn't find anything that showed a trace of Luke.

I ran faster and faster; only to stumble into a small park. I wasn't quite sure if it should have been there. I looked around frantically to find Luke being thrown over the shoulder of a figure that I barely could make out. It was dark and even seeing my brother was a task on its own. Confusion crossed his face. He fought and screamed the moment that he realized what was happening.

"Let me go!" He commanded as he kicked the

man in the stomach. The man bent down in pain. Luke pulled the man's hair and struggled.

I ran up behind the man and jumped on his back while he was still doubled over. I gripped his neck and pulled back with all my strength. The man stumbled backwards, hitting me into the wall. I didn't let go but held on his neck to try to stop him from breathing. Luke bit into the skin between his neck and shoulder.

The man cried out in pain as he dropped Luke. My brother's head bounced off the concrete; a large crack seemed to thunder through the park. I scooped up my brother, grabbing the bag next to him and raced down the alleyway across from us. Luke's weight slowed me down greatly, but I pushed on. I focused on running away from the shadowed man that I could hear was standing up. I had to lose him somehow! I took a right, and my feet slipped under me. I placed my empty hand on the ground, scraping the skin, and kept my feet from running away. I got up and kept running, trying not to lose momentum.

I sent out another prayer, begging for safety. I rounded another corner and pressed myself against the wall, hugging Luke's unconscious body to my chest. A soft pattering rang loudly in the empty alley. I listened closely but there were no footsteps. I let out a relieved breath and carefully put Luke on the ground. I brushed his mop of black hair out of his eyes.

I softly shook him, trying to wake him up. I brushed his hair back again only to feel something sticky. I pulled my hand away to find a dark liquid covering a few of my fingers. I panicked and frantically looked around. I was told that head damage was deadly.

I dug around in his bag and pulled out a nice button up shirt. I grabbed the kitchen knife we stashed away and used it to tear the sleeve away from the rest of the shirt. I put the knife down and grabbed a bottle of water. I carefully wet it and patted the area where the wound might be; then I tied the opposite side around Luke's head.

I pressed my ear to my twin's chest and listened closely. A soft thumping announced that Luke was still alive and okay for now. I put the bag on my back and look around. I ran straight into a dead end. The only choice was to go back. Maybe one of the side streets led to the road? As I got ready to pick Luke up, I heard footsteps walking toward me.

I pushed myself close to my brother. Fear pledged my entire body. I pulled Luke into my arms and dragged him away from the towering figure. I watched him bend over to pick up the stolen knife from the ground. He carefully looked at it.

"Dad…" I whispered my soft plead. I needed to be forgiven! Luke couldn't be harmed anymore. Father loomed over us, looking me deep in my eyes. His emerald eyes seemed darker than the night around us. I couldn't breathe at this point. My throat was choked up with pure fear. I looked him over and noticed that his right shoulder was bleeding. Father's shirt was soaked in blood. How was he still standing?

"Don't be scared" He talked softly. A rich, deep voice growled out under his pain filled one. It wasn't him anymore. He lost too much blood. It wasn't him. "It's just me, your poor, unloved, misunderstood son, Papa."

I ended up hitting my back on a wall. I pushed Luke away from me as I watched Father pull something glittery out of his waistband. My heart stopped, and my gut churned.

A scream ripped through the air. Who screamed? It sounded close. Oh, the ground; the ground was cool and so pretty. I never told anyone but I loved the color red. It was pretty, spreading out on the ground. My chest felt empty. My head was filled with fluff. I wanted to see Luke's joy-filled face one more time. Maybe, I could push him on the swings in the park one day. Graduation would be fun one day. We were going to see Mom soon, I guessed. I needed to say that I was sorry. Oh, and the angels. I needed to go find the girls once I got past Father.

Wow, was I always that tired?

18: Once I Let Go

Alice

I FELT MY heart stop. I rolled over and looked around, what was going on? A hand pulled me toward the car door. I slowly got out, making sure not to get hit by any passing cars. This was not the safest place in the world. I slowly walked up the sidewalk. I noticed a child's voice in the distance. It was so soft that I couldn't tell what it was saying, but I began running. I turned around a corner to find Arthur standing over Ryan's bleeding body; smoke raised out of the gun that he held in his right hand.

I put my hand in my pocket and reached around for my phone. I hit the emergency contact button. I felt it vibrating in my pocket. Come on, pick up. The phone stopped ringing, and someone was mumbling in my pocket. "Arthur!" I screamed at the top of my lungs, "How dare you shoot them!" My husband whirled around and glared at me.

"Ah, Alice found the rabbit," Arthur spoke slowly, punctuating each word with a small pop. Not Arthur. No, that's not his voice. Not even drunk his voice that was filled with that much malice.

"Too bad Tweedle Dee and Tweedle Dum aren't up and about, how about meeting with the Hatter?" His grin grew, splitting his face in two. What is he?

I looked past whatever he was. Ryan laid sideways on the ground; his breaths labored, Luke's body was across from him, his eyes flittering open slightly. I reached down to where I kept the gun, but it wasn't there. I gritted my teeth and grabbed my phone out of my pocket; it was still on call with the police. I dared to look down to make sure.

P-taff!

I immediately ducked down and put my hands over my head. My ears rang. I opened my eyes after a few seconds to find that I wasn't shot, Arthur was. I slowly got up and looked around to find my own smoking gun on the ground. I felt my heart start beating once more as I looked at Arthur; his face was so pale, and he lost so much blood from the first time I shot him. It wasn't my problem anymore.

I pushed past Arthur, kicking him with my shoe and gathered Ryan in my arms. I gave him a quick look over. The bullet hit him in the throat; he had to be chocking on his own blood. I brushed his black hair back. "Don't die, baby. Mamma's here for you." I begged him, holding him to my chest.

I looked over and grabbed Luke, holding them

like babies. Luke looked slightly lucid. I kissed the top of his head, making sure not to disturb the makeshift bandage. Burning tears streamed down my face as I looked between my two boys. I held them close. "Please God, send someone for me. Let them live; please let them live." I begged the air. I pulled my boys' closer, my chest covered in Ryan's blood. *'Someone help us.'* Luke grabbed his brother's hand tightly as his eyes closed again.

"No, please! Stay awake for mommy!" I begged him. "Please, don't do this to me! Please, just give me another chance!"

Footsteps echoed through the empty alleyway. A small girl walked toward us. Her hair hung loosely; her white gown blew delicately in the wind. Bright red wings blocked out the alley that she appeared in. She faded in herself, the wings being the only thing that made me realize that she truly was there. She walked next to Arthur; the blood covering the ground never picked up on her bare feet. She leaned down and brushed my check, catching my tears with her finger. My throat tightened up, but the rest of my body relaxed.

The strange girl didn't speak as she put a small iris in Ryan's hair and handed me a raspberry blossom. I found my voice blocked as she placed a silver necklace with an ocean blue pendant around Luke's neck and put a black and a red feather in his hand, along with a golden necklace with a red pendant. She looked at me, her eyes promising a new life, a new home, and a new hope. I closed my eyes as I felt her hand brush over my face and her kiss on my forehead. Once I opened my lids, the girl was gone. Around me, I could hear the sirens of a police car.

I pulled the boys close to my chest as I slowly stood up and made my way to the car.

19: I Will Finally Breath Free

Luke

I SAT UP in bed, drenched in sweat and the phantom feeling of Ryan's hand still in mine. I reached up and clutched the pendant around my neck. A wave of calm filled me as I looked around trying to get my bearings. The empty bed across the room was neatly made as it always will be. The baby blue room with its bright lights was still dark. The sun had yet to raise. Clothes weren't scattered on the floor anymore. Boxes lined the walls.

Every little change set my heart down into my gut. My heart tightened, and my throat constricted. I tried to calm my racing heart. I couldn't give up that early. I looked over at my alarm clock which woke me up. Soft music was still playing on it. It sounded like a strange blur between Moonlight and Symphony no. 9. I pressed the stop button and pushed back my sheets.

I started making my bed as I heard a soft knock on the door. I walked over, dodging papers that were thrown around in a fury. Stories upon stories that Ryan and I wrote together were torn up and abandoned, waiting to be swept up or vacuumed away. I didn't dare touch the toys that we had yet to pack.

I opened the door, the cold metal of the knob burning my hand. I paused for a moment, fear swelled my heart. I just wanted to stay in bed. I opened the door slightly to see Mother fidgeting with her hands behind the door. I relaxed and opened the door all the way.

"Luke? May I come in?" the raven-haired women softly asked.

I nodded, stepping to the side to allow Mother into my room. "Sweetheart. You need to get dressed; today is the day."

Her face was solemn. She was dressed in black with a navy blue sash tied at the waist. I nodded again. I took a glace toward the wardrobe that was hiding my outfit. She ran her hand through my mop of black hair and sighed. "Take your time, Luke," she said, then she made her way to the door, closing it behind her.

I felt my chest burn. Guilt laid a heavy hand on my heart as I went through the closet to find the new clothes. I slowly got dressed in the black slacks. I buttoned up the shirt, each one taking agonizingly slow. I didn't bother with the coat that was supposed to go over the white shirt. I pulled the silver necklace out from under the collar. I closed the closet and looked around the room. That day was the last time I saw that room. I could barely believe it.

I took a feather from the dresser that held my alarm clock. I brushed the black feather back and held it close to my heart. I had to keep it safe. I pocketed the feather and looked around once more. Memories of laughing, crying, and hiding filled my mind. Every corner of this room was filled with so many emotions; the air was suffocating, but it felt wonderful. I took a breath and walked out of the room. I slowly closed the door behind me, small pings of pain ran their course but no tears formed. I slowly moved away from the room and down the small hallway, into the living room. Bright colors stood out against the mood like they didn't belong.

"Ready to go?" Mom asked me as I entered the room.

I looked around once more, then lowered my eyes down to my clean hands. I looked at her and nodded. She smiled sadly and led me to the car. It was a red sports car. I watched as we pulled away from the house I lived in for years. Bricks made it look like a normal place. The lawn was as perfect as the flowers that grew there. The drive was silent, as most of our days were. No one ever said anything anymore. I knew I should have been the one in his place. Not him. Why did Father go after my brother?

The cemetery was empty when we pulled up. There would never be a huge mourning thing; it would just be us there. We pulled into the parking lot in front of the church. Mother parked and looked out past everything. It was an ocean of stones. There were statues of angels and praying children. A whole place full of children's graves.

Slowly, we both climbed out of the car. We walked in silence past all the graves. Some names and graves were old, but some were new. And one was freshly placed back into its original spot. We stopped in front of Ryan's grave. A small stone marked his resting place. A multitude of flowers rested on the grave.

There were white orchids, roses of light pink,

deep red, and white. Bouquets and single flowers laid around, slowly rotting away. I felt frustration boil in my gut. I balled my hands to fists and resisted the urge to kick those hideous flowers. Ryan hated flowers. He thought they were too girly for him. I always disagreed but now seeing them laid out; I couldn't help but hate them too.

Mother couldn't even look at where her lost son laid, so she looked away at the parking lot. I could always tell that she rather had Ryan there instead of me. She never wanted me. Ryan was the good kid, huh? She blamed me for his death, didn't she?

"I'll leave you to yourself," Mom told me, then she turned and walked away.

I looked down at the book. Three months now. Three months have gone by since his death. I was unable to remember the days after nor the days that led up to this moment. It was just strange, getting up in the morning, going down for breakfast, going to school, everything without Ryan. I didn't even show up for his funeral. What a horrible brother I was. Ran off, let him die and didn't even show up to properly send him off.

I bent down and brushed the flowers off the headstone. The feeling to kick them still lingered, but slowly faded. I dug through my pocket and found some stones. Each of them was a different size and color. My favorite and the largest one was a darkish green. Something about it felt right. I slowly placed them under the stone book in a tight circle. The rocks formed a roundabout from biggest to smallest, darkest to lightest. I stood back up and looked down at them. Everything about the circle felt perfect.

I ended up kicking the flowers away. They were dead. What was the deal if they were gone? Flowers faded too quickly; their beauty was just us being told that they meant something. But rocks, rocks lasted for a long time. Rocks could shine brighter than any flower when seen the perfect angle in the light. That's what Ryan was, the largest rock on the side of the beach. He just got washed away to a new adventure. A new beginning. Something. He had to be doing something new. I was unable to wrap my head around him being completely gone.

"Ryan?" I whispered. I felt my throat closing up, telling me not to speak, "This is really strange, but if you can hear me, please know that I love you. I love you. I can't live without you!" I felt a tear slipping down my checks, "Please, brother! Don't leave me!" I bent over, my head hurt, and my heart beat loudly. My eyes burned, but I could not cry! Let me cry, please!

"Luke?" I whipped my head up; panic and shame grabbed hold of me. Kimmy and Angela were standing behind me. I bit my lip to keep from screaming. They looked at each other with worried expressions on their faces. God, I hated that look! I got that very same look from every adult! The girls started toward me, their white hair shimmering in the summer sunlight.

I cringed away from them and looked down, quickly wiping my tears away. I couldn't hold my head up to them. But why was I embarrassed to see them? They should be hanging their heads! Yet, here I was; hanging my head like a disobedient child.

"Luke, we're sorry," Angela said very carefully, "We couldn't go against orders, but we tried as hard as we could. We wanted to help!" I felt my teeth bite too hard, drawing blood from my lip. My fist trembled. The need to hit them grabbed my throat and held my wrist. My breathing was controlled by someone else. They continued talking. Their voices were so annoying!

I just wanted them to go away! Go away! "Just Go AWAY!"

They paused, Kimmy was in the middle of talking, and her mouth hung open with surprise. I breathed heavily. I didn't plan to scream it out, but if they would go away, I didn't care.

"Luke?" Kimmy asked softly. Angela glared at me, grabbing her sister's arm.

"Come on, Kimmy. He doesn't want help." Angela turned Kimmy away from me. They slowly walked away.

I hung my head once more and looked at Ryan's grave. I slowly sat next to the stone. I pulled my knees to my chest. I wanted to cry so much, but no tears were falling. I played with the small pendant on my neck. It burned in my hand.

A small hand is placed on my shoulder. I jolted up, looking around, but no one was there. I sighed and laughed softly. Wow, I was going crazy. I slowly brushed my hair back; my hand caught something. I pulled it loose and look down to find a red string wrapped around my fingers.

"Luke." Mother called from the parking lot. I

slowly made my way away from my brother's resting place. I played with the string for a while, but once I got to the car, I dropped it and stomped on it. I climbed into the car and buckled my seat belt.

Mother pulled the car out of the parking lot.

Author's Note

I know you hear, *__it will get better__* but trust me it will. Someone does want you to live. And if someone tells you to go kill yourself, please do not listen to them. If you are depressed go talk to someone! It makes **you** feel better, even if not your problem, but if they make you laugh or even take your mind off it, somehow it will make you feel, even a tiny bit, better.

Thank you for reading my book.

1 (800) 273-8255

suicidepreventionlifeline.org

National Suicide Prevention Lifeline

Hours: 24 hours, 7 days a week

Languages English and Spanish.

1-800-run-away

(1-800-786-2929)

www.1800runaway.org

National Runaway Safe line

www.ingramcontent.com/pod-product-compliance
Lightning Source LLC
Chambersburg PA
CBHW020917180626
46816CB00007BA/2442